SORRY
(REALLY SORRY)

Words by JOANNA COTLER
Pictures by HARRY BLISS

PHILOMEL BOOKS

Thank you Elena, Ellery, Harry, Holly and Jill.—J.C.

PHILOMEL BOOKS
An imprint of Penguin Random House LLC
New York

First published in the United States of America by Philomel,
an imprint of Penguin Random House LLC, 2020.

Visit us online at penguinrandomhouse.com

Library of Congress Cataloging-in-Publication Data is available upon request
Manufactured in China by RR Donnelley Asia Printing Solutions Ltd.
ISBN 9781984812476
1 2 3 4 5 6 7 8 9 10

Edited by Jill Santopolo.
Design by Ellice M. Lee.
Text set in Clarendom Com.
The art was done in black India ink and watercolor.

For Mark, with so much love—J.C.

For John Butler—H.B.

Cow was in a nasty mood. Usually she was content to munch grass, rub up against fences, and play with her farm friends. But it had rained the night before, and this morning her hooves were deep in mud. That made her mad.

When Duck came along, Cow kicked
mud in her face.

"Why'd you do that?" asked Duck.

"I felt like it," said Cow. "And I'm not sorry."

Flapping furiously, Duck
wiped mud from her beak.

"Hi, Duck," said Frog. "You're all muddy. Want to swim with me?"

Duck thought of how mean Cow had been. "No, you gross green glob!"

"Am not," said Frog.

"Are too," said Duck.

"Say you're sorry," said Frog.

"Sorry," said Duck.

"Not sorry" is
what she meant,
and Frog knew it.

Frog was angry.

I might be green, but I'm no glob, Frog thought.

Bird sang out her best song,
hoping to cheer Frog up.

Frog said, "Tweet, tweet, tweet, your tweets stink!"

"Hey! Why'd you say that?" asked Bird.

"I felt like it," said Frog.

Bird's feelings were hurt. She thought her tweets were lovely.

"Aren't you even sorry?" asked Bird.

"Sorry," said Frog.
But he wasn't sorry.
Not one bit.

Bird flew up into a tree.
There was Goat, perched on a branch.

"This is my
branch," said
Bird. "Get down!"

"But we always
share this tree,"
said Goat.

"Not anymore," said Bird, and she beat her wings until Goat tumbled to the ground.

And she wasn't sorry. Not at all.

Goat ran as fast as he could. He wanted to get away from Bird.

He ran so fast, he ran right into Pig.

"Ow," said Pig.

"I did that on purpose," said Goat,
even though he hadn't.

"Why?" asked Pig.

"I felt like it. And I'm not
sorry," said Goat.

Pig lay down in the farmyard and began to cry—

big,
    loud,
        honking
            snorts.

"What's wrong?" asked Dog.

"Go away. I don't even like you," said Pig.

Pig honked and snorted some more.

Dog just sat
there and let Pig
cry for a while.

Dog said, "I know you like me. We eat lunch together every day."

"That's true," sniffed Pig.

"And sometimes you even share your favorite, waffles," said Dog.

"I do love waffles," sniffed Pig.

"Goat was mean to me so I got
mad. Sorry," said Pig.
And she meant it.
"Okay," said Dog.

Dog gave Pig a big, long lick.

Pig felt better. So . . .

Pig found Goat and gave him a nuzzle.

The nuzzle made Goat feel so good he brought Bird a delicious snack, a worm sandwich.

And . . .

Bird, who couldn't find Frog, left a box of flies with a note that said, "I love you, Frog!"

When Frog got Bird's note, he found Duck and went to swim in the pond with her.

And there was Cow,
who had started it all.

"Cow," said Duck. "Want to play with me and Frog?"

"Yes, I would," said Cow, walking into the pond.

"Duck, I am sorry I kicked mud on you."

And she was sorry. Really, truly sorry.

"Why'd you do that?" asked Duck.

"I don't like muddy hooves," said Cow.

"Better now?" asked Duck.

"Better now," said Cow.

And she was, until . . .

Horse was surrounded by flies . . .